Henny Penny

First published in Great Britain in 2006 by Bloomsbury Publishing Plc
36 Soho Square, London, W1D 3QY

This paperback edition first published in 2007

A CIP catalogue record of this book is available from the British Library

ISBN 978 0 7475 8104 8

Printed in China by South China Printing Co

1 3 5 7 9 10 8 6 4 2

All papers used by Bloomsbury Publishing are natural, recyclable products made from wood grown in well-managed forests.
The manufacturing processes conform to the environmental regulations of the country of origin.

Henny Penny

Vivian French & Sophie Windham

BLOOMSBURY
CHILDREN'S
BOOKS

For Simon with much love
V.F.

For Willow
S.W.

Now, you may already have heard the story of Henny Penny ... and you may have been told how her foolishness led her to a terrible end. That, I promise you, is not the real story. That is the story the foxes like to tell. This is the true story, the story of what really happened after the acorn fell from the oak tree.

How do I know?
Because Henny Penny told me.

Henny Penny was busy in her kitchen making a big corn cake.

She mixed it, and she whisked it, and she stirred it, and she put it
in the oven to cook.

"There," said Henny Penny, "what a delicious cake that will be! But, oh dear
me! There's cornflour everywhere!" And she picked up a duster
and began to dust.

"ATCHOO!" sneezed
Henny Penny.
"ATCHOO! I must
take my duster outside
and shake it."

She hurried outside to shake
her duster this way and that
way and round and round, and
as she was shaking it ...

PLOP!

An acorn fell from the oak tree and landed on Henny Penny's head.

"Cluck, cluck, CLUCK!" squawked Henny Penny. "Oh, my goodness, and mercy, mercy me! I do believe the sky is falling down ...

Whatever shall I do? I must go and tell the king!"
And Henny Penny stuffed her duster into her pocket and set off along the road.

She hadn't gone far when she met Ducky Lucky.
"Hello, Henny Penny," said Ducky Lucky. "You look to be in a terrible hurry.
Where are you going?"

"Oh, Ducky Lucky!" said Henny Penny. "I was shaking my duster this way and
that way and round and round, and all of a sudden the sky fell down!
And I don't know what to do, so I'm going to tell the king."

"Quack, quack, QUACK!" quacked Ducky Lucky. "If the sky is falling down I'd better come with you."

So Henny Penny and Ducky Lucky pit-pit-pattered along the road together.

They hadn't gone very far when they met Cocky Locky.

"Hello, Henny Penny," said Cocky Locky. "Hello, Ducky Lucky. You look to be in a terrible hurry. Where are you going?"

"Oh, Cocky Locky!" said Henny Penny. "I was shaking my duster this way and that way and round and round, and all of a sudden the sky fell down! And I don't know what to do, so we're going to tell the king."

"Cock-a-doodle-DOO!" crowed Cocky Locky. "If the sky is falling down I'd better come with you."

So Henny Penny, Ducky Lucky and Cocky Locky pit-pit-pattered along the road together.

They hadn't gone far when they met Goosey Loosey.
"Hello, Henny Penny," said Goosey Loosey. "Hello, Ducky Lucky and Cocky Locky.
You look to be in a terrible hurry. Where are you going?"

"Oh, Goosey Loosey!" said Henny Penny. "I was shaking my duster this
way and that way and round and round, and all of a sudden the sky fell
down! And I don't know what to do, so we're going to tell the king."

"Hiss, hiss, HISS!" hissed Goosey Loosey.
"If the sky is falling down, I'd better come with you."

So Henny Penny, Ducky Lucky, Cocky
Locky and Goosey Loosey
pit-pit-pattered along
the road together.

They hadn't gone far when they met Turkey Lurkey.
"Hello, Henny Penny," said Turkey Lurkey. "Hello, Ducky Lucky, and Cocky
Locky, and Goosey Loosey. You look to be in a terrible hurry.
Where are you going?"

"Oh, Turkey Lurkey!" said Henny Penny. "I was shaking my duster this way
and that way and round and round, and all of a sudden the sky fell down! And
I don't know what to do, so we're going to tell the king."

"Gobble, gobble, GOBBLE!" gobbled Turkey Lurkey. "If the sky is falling down I'd better come with you."

So Henny Penny, Ducky Lucky, Cocky Locky, Goosey Loosey and Turkey Lurkey pit-pit-pattered along the road together.

They hadn't gone far when they met Foxy Loxy.

"Well, well, well," said Foxy Loxy, "and who have we here? Henny Penny, Ducky Lucky,
Cocky Locky, Goosey Loosey and Turkey Lurkey, if my old eyes don't deceive me.
And where are you going in such a hurry?"

"Oh, Foxy Loxy!" said Henny Penny. "I was shaking my duster this way and that way
and round and round, and all of a sudden the sky fell down!
And we don't know what to do, so we're going to tell the king."

"What a sensible Henny Penny you are," said Foxy Loxy, and he smiled a sharp-toothed smile. "And do you know which way to go?"

Henny Penny stopped and thought about it.

"How silly I am," she said. "No, I don't!"

"Then do let me show you," said Foxy Loxy. "Just follow me."

So Henny Penny, Ducky Lucky, Cocky Locky, Goosey Loosey
and Turkey Lurkey pit-pit-pattered after Foxy Loxy.

And Foxy Loxy led them through the grass ...

and under the trees ...

and in and out of the bushes ...

until suddenly ...

there they were in a dusty musty kitchen, in a dusty musty
house, and Foxy Loxy was shutting the door behind them.

"Gobble, gobble, gobble!" said Turkey Lurkey.
"Is this where the king lives?"
"No, my dears," said Foxy Loxy. "This is MY house. I thought
we could all have a lovely dinner before we go to see the king.
Just sit yourselves down, and I'll light the fire."

Ducky Lucky settled down on the hearth mat.
Cocky Locky perched on a chair.
Goosey Loosey and Turkey Lurkey flapped up to the sofa.

Henny Penny stood very still, and looked around.

She saw the feathers on the floor.

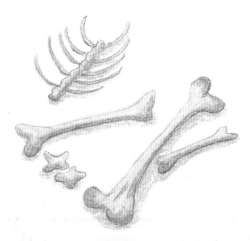

She saw the pile of old bones in the corner.

She saw Foxy Loxy putting a BIG pan of water on the roaring fire ...

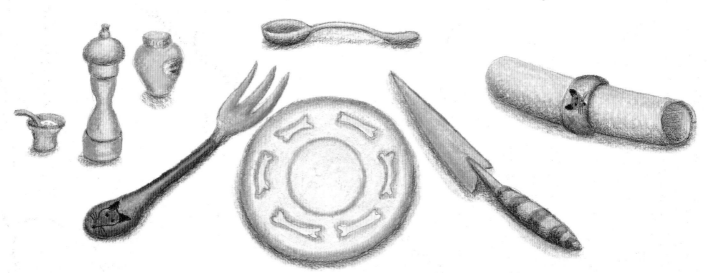

and she saw him lay the table with one fork, and one spoon, and one big sharp knife.

Henny Penny felt pale, but she shook her head and she fluffed up her feathers. "Now, Henny Penny," she said to herself. "You may be a silly Henny Penny, but there's sure to be something you can do."

And Henny Penny
had an idea.

"Oh, Mr Fox!" said Henny Penny. "What a mess! What a muddle! DO let me tidy it up!"
And she pulled her duster out of her pocket.
Foxy Loxy was MOST surprised. "Eh, WHAT?" he said.

Ducky Lucky, Cocky Locky, Goosey Loosey and Turkey Lurkey stared at Henny Penny.
"Gobble, gobble, gobble! What about our tea?" said Turkey Lurkey.

"Let's make Mr Fox comfortable first," Henny Penny said. "Now, Mr Fox,
you sit down and take a little rest, and I'll give your room a polish and shine.
We'll wake you up when it's clean and tidy."
Foxy Loxy stroked his whiskers. His house certainly was rather messy,
now he came to look at it.

"Very well, then," he said. "But be sure to wake me the
moment you've finished!"
"Gobble, gobble, gobble!" said Turkey Lurkey. "Then we'll all have tea!"
"We certainly will," said Foxy Loxy, and he licked his lips as
he sat himself down in his comfiest chair.

Henny Penny began to dust. As she dusted she began to sing:
"*Hush, Mr Foxy, and close your eyes ...*
Soon you'll be having a special surprise ..."
"Gobble, gobble, gobble!" said Turkey Lurkey. "Will we have a surprise too?"

Foxy Loxy opened one eye. "Oh, yes," he said, and his belly rumbled.
"You'll have a BIG surprise, Turkey Lurkey!"

"Shh, Turkey Lurkey!" said Henny Penny, and she went on dusting and singing.

"Hush, Mr Foxy, and close your eyes ...

Soon you'll be having a special surprise ..."

Foxy Loxy sighed, and closed his eyes.

Henny Penny went on dusting and singing.

Foxy Loxy began to snore.

Henny Penny went on singing, but she quietly,
quietly, quietly opened the door ...
and Ducky Lucky, Cocky Locky and Goosey
Loosey tiptoed out.
"Gobble, gobble, gobble!" said Turkey Lurkey.
"What about my surprise?"

Foxy Loxy grunted in his sleep.
"Turkey Lurkey," whispered Henny Penny,
"if you don't tiptoe out, Mr Fox
will give you a great, big, TERRIBLE
surprise - he'll eat you for his dinner!"

"GOBBLE, GOBBLE, GOBBLE!" shouted Turkey Lurkey, and he flapped, and he flurried, and he flounced through the door just as fast as he could go, and Henny Penny flew after him ...

and Foxy Loxy woke up just as the door banged shut behind them both.

Turkey Lurkey, Goosey Loosey, Cocky Locky and
Ducky Lucky didn't say anything at all until they reached Henny
Penny's house. There was a wonderful smell of corn cake as Henny
Penny opened the door and let them in.

"I don't think we'll bother the king today," Henny Penny said.
"Let's have a slice of corn cake instead."

And that, as Turkey Lurkey said, was the best surprise of all.